Dear Parent:
Your child's love of reading

T0253312

Every child learns to read in a different way
speed. Some go back and forth between reading levels and read
favorite books again and again. Others read through each level in
order. You can help your young reader improve and become more
confident by encouraging his or her own interests and abilities. From
books your child reads with you to the first books he or she reads
alone, there are I Can Read Books for every stage of reading:

SHARED READING
Basic language, word repetition, and whimsical illustrations,
ideal for sharing with your emergent reader

BEGINNING READING
Short sentences, familiar words, and simple concepts
for children eager to read on their own

READING WITH HELP
Engaging stories, longer sentences, and language play
for developing readers

READING ALONE
Complex plots, challenging vocabulary, and high-interest topics
for the independent reader

ADVANCED READING
Short paragraphs, chapters, and exciting themes
for the perfect bridge to chapter books

I Can Read Books have introduced children to the joy of reading
since 1957. Featuring award-winning authors and illustrators and a
fabulous cast of beloved characters, I Can Read Books set the
standard for beginning readers.

A lifetime of discovery begins with the magical words **"I Can Read!"**

Visit www.icanread.com for information
on enriching your child's reading experience.

How to Drive Your Sister Crazy

story by Diane Z. Shore
pictures by Laura Rankin

HARPER

An Imprint of HarperCollinsPublishers

To my son,
Samuel Lawrence Shore,
the real Bradley Harris Pinkerton
—D.Z.S.

To my sister, who in our youth
was forced to say to me daily,
"Quit it or I'll pound you!"
—L.R.

How to Drive Your Sister Crazy Text copyright © 2008 by Diane Z. Shore Illustrations copyright © 2008 by Laura Rankin All rights reserved. No part of this book may be used or reproduced in any manner whatsoever without written permission except in the case of brief quotations embodied in critical articles and reviews. Printed in the U.S.A. For information address HarperCollins Children's Books, a division of HarperCollins Publishers, 195 Broadway, New York, NY 10007. www.icanread.com

Library of Congress Cataloging-in-Publication Data is available.
ISBN 978-0-06-052762-4 (trade bdg.) — ISBN 978-0-06-052764-8 (pbk.)

23 24 CWM 20   ❖   First Edition

CONTENTS

How to Drive Your Sister

CRAZY

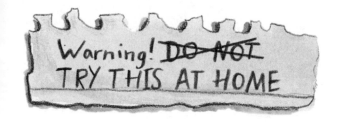

Warning! ~~DO NOT~~ TRY THIS AT HOME

Do you have a big sister?

Do you know how to drive her crazy?

It's easy, really easy.

Take it from me,

Bradley Harris Pinkerton.

I'm good at it.

Just ask my sister, Abby.

NOTE: *It's your job*

to drive your sister crazy.

You might as well do it right.

1. Hide and Ssseek

Most likely your sister

lives in the bathroom.

(That means she spends

a lot of time there.)

This is perfect.

There are lots of ways

to drive your sister crazy

when she's in the bathroom.

First, knock on the door.

Your sister will say something like,

"Get lost! I'm in the shower!"

"But I can't find Slimey," you say.

"Who is Slimey!?" she will ask.

Slimey is your new rubber snake.

But do not tell your sister that.

Just say, "He's the snake I found. . . ."

"AAAUGH!!" your sister will scream.

She will unlock the door

and jump back into the shower.

Now walk in. Hiss like a snake.

"Sssss! Did you hear that?" you say.

Your sister will peek from behind

the shower curtain.

"Get that snake out of here!"

she will yell.

"No problem," you say.

Now get on your hands and knees.

Look for Slimey behind the toilet.

Your sister will peek from behind
the shower curtain again.
"DID YOU FIND HIM?!"
she will yell.
"No," you tell her. "The only thing
behind the toilet is dirt."
Now your hands are dirty.
This is perfect.
Brush your hands together and say,
"I need to wash my hands."
"NO!" she'll cry.
"Don't turn on the—"

Turn on the hot water in the sink.

"AAAAUGH!" your sister will scream.

When you turn on
the hot water in the sink,
the water in the shower
turns really cold.

"Oops, sorry," you say.

NOTE: *Watch for flying soap.*

"Get out! Now!!" she will yell.

"Sure thing," you say.

On your way out, grab her towel,

turn out the lights,

and hiss like a snake, "Sssssss!"

This will drive your sister crazy.

She will yell your full name.

"BRATLEY HARRIS PINKERTON!"

(Or something close

to your full name.)

Do not answer.

Your sister will jump out of the shower

and turn on the lights.

"Where's my towel?!"

she will scream,

and run to the hall closet

for another one.

When she opens the closet door,

she will scream again,

"AAAAAAUGH!!"

because Slimey is waiting in the closet.

By now you will be in your

special hiding place.

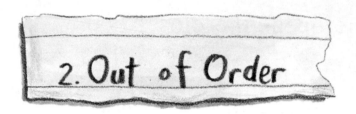

2. Out of Order

Most likely your sister has a sign

on her bedroom door.

It says something like:

And most likely you do the opposite

of what your sister tells you to do.

This is perfect.

If you do the opposite of what your sister tells you to do, then you'll read the sign like this:

So you do.

NOTE: *Make sure your sister is in the bathroom.*

Everything in your sister's bedroom
has its own special place—
the purple hairbrush on her dresser,

the purple teddy bears on her bed,

and the purple alarm clock
on her nightstand.
Notice the chewed bubble gum
next to the purple alarm clock.
(Guess what color?)

Now, this part is very important.
Set the alarm clock
for 3:00 in the morning, and put it
in your sister's underwear drawer.
NOTE: *Do NOT touch her underpants!*
Yuck!

Now stick her hairbrush

in the pencil holder on her desk.

Put the purple teddy bears

on the ceiling fan.

Take the piece of chewed bubble gum

and stick it on the light switch

(which also turns on the ceiling fan).

Put the gum wrapper in your pocket.

Now everything is out of order.

This will drive your sister crazy.

Your sister will come

into her bedroom.

The first thing she will do

is turn on the light switch

(which also turns on the fan).

"AAAUGH!!" your sister will scream

as she dodges the teddy bears

flying across the room.

Then your sister
will look at her hand.
"YUCK!!" she will scream,
because the gum is still wet
from when you tasted it.

She will yell your full name.

"BRATley **HAIRBRAIN** Pinkerton!"

(Or something close

to your full name.)

Do not answer.

By now you will be

in your special hiding place.

3. Phone Fun

Most likely your sister
has two best friends:
another girl and the telephone.
(That means she spends
a lot of time on the phone.)

This is perfect.

The best time to drive

your sister crazy

is when her best friend calls.

This will drive her best friend

crazy too.

Always be the first
to answer the phone.
Answer in a really deep voice:
"Hello, Flopsy's Rabbit Ranch.
What's *hop*pening?"

"Very funny, Bradley,"
your sister's best friend will say.
"No," you say. "It's very BUNNY!"
Then hang up.

The phone will ring again.

It will be you-know-who.

This time let your sister answer.

Now, this part is very important.
You must pick up another phone
in another room at the same time
your sister picks up her phone.

Your sister's best friend
will start talking.
She will say something like,
"Your little brother is so . . ."

Remember the gum wrapper
in your pocket?

Take it out now and crinkle it.

"What?" your sister will say.

"I didn't hear you."

As your sister is talking,

tiptoe upstairs to her bedroom.

NOTE: *DO NOT let her see you.*

Your sister's best friend
will say again, "I said,
your little brother is so . . ."
Crinkle the gum wrapper again,
then sneak a little closer
to your sister.

"WHAT?" your sister will say.

Sneak up closer.

Closer.

Your sister's best friend

will say again,

"I SAID, YOUR LITTLE BROTHER

IS SO . . ."

Jump into your sister's bedroom.

"PERFECT!!" you yell.

"AAAUGH!!" your sister will scream.

She will yell your full name.

"BRAT*LEY *HAIRBRAIN

***STINK*ERTON!"**

(Or something close to your full name.)

Drop the phone and run

to your special hiding place.

4. Heart to Heart

Sneak out of your

special hiding place.

NOTE: *Make sure your sister*

is in the bathroom.

Go to your sister's desk.

Write a note.

Write something like this

Now, this part is very important.

Color the heart purple.

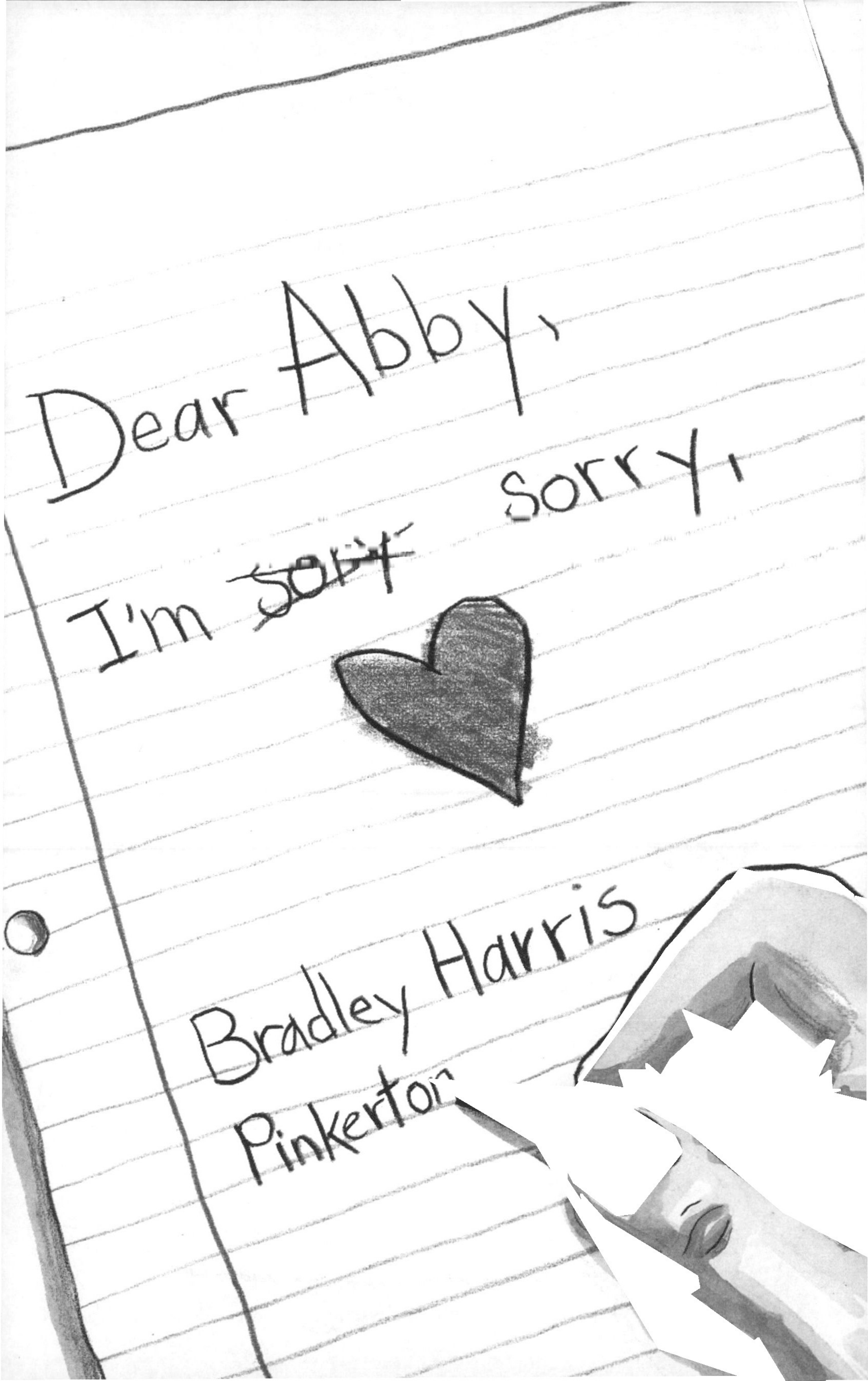
Dear Abby,
I'm ~~sory~~ sorry,
Bradley Harris
Pinkerton

Leave the note
next to her hairbrush.
(Her hairbrush will be
back on her dresser by now.)
Sneak back to your
special hiding place.

When your sister sees the heart

she will forget everything.

Now it is safe to come out

of your hiding place . . .

until 3:00 in the morning,
when your sister's underpants
start ringing.